Moya and the Flamingoes

Other Books by EMILY W. HALLIN

With Robert Buell
FOLLOW THE HONEY BIRD
WILD WHITE WINGS

MOYA AND THE FLAMINGOES

by
Emily W. Hallin

Illustrated by Rus Anderson

DAVID McKAY COMPANY, INC.
New York
1969

MOYA AND THE FLAMINGOES

COPYRIGHT © 1969 BY

EMILY HALLIN

LIBRARY OF CONGRESS CATALOG CARD NUMBER: 69–12953

MANUFACTURED IN THE UNITED STATES OF AMERICA

CONTENTS

Moya and the Flamingoes

1: A Discovery

Moya was the first to see that the flamingoes had come to build their nests.

In the early morning, he was sitting upon his platform in the acacia tree by his father's millet field. Beside him was a pyramid of stones. Whenever birds settled in the millet field, Moya threw a stone to frighten them away. The millet was almost ready for harvesting, and Moya and his brothers took turns protecting it from the birds.

As he waited on his platform, Moya saw a wild pig run beside the field. Although he should have stayed on his platform until the shadow of the acacia tree had reached a certain point in the field, Moya could not resist the pig. He reached for the branch above him, grabbed it with both hands, twisted his body forward, and dropped to the ground. He was off after the wild pig that rustled the dry, gray-green leaves of the leleshwa bushes as it scuttled through.

The pig scurried down the steep ravines in the rocky cliffs

where the earth had once cracked apart to form the Rift Valley. At last, when Moya, confused by the noises of other small creatures in the underbrush, lost track of the pig, he had run a long distance from home. He had reached a point where a spring bubbled from the cliffs of the Rift wall and made a clear stream of water running into an azure lake ringed by a snow white rim. He was all the way to the Lake of the Firebirds!

Moya did not often come to this lake, for the sun blazed from the brilliant crust about the water like a hot coal of fire touching one's skin, and the liquid was bitter and sluggish. He and his friends had tried some one day when they were thirsty. It had a horrible taste.

"It's poison!" Moya had cried, and he asked Kimani, his oldest brother, if they would all die of it. But Kimani had led them to the fresh water spring to rinse the bad taste from their mouths. Now, remembering that day, Moya smelled the foul vapor arising from the lake, and it made his stomach churn and his head dizzy.

There was a secret cave near the spring which only Moya and his brothers knew, but they seldom played there. They preferred the cool shade of the forests near their homes.

Besides, it was dangerous to play near the flamingoes, for they were wild, strange creatures, and easily frightened.

It was said that long ago, Ngai, the god of Moya's clan, had sent fire to man on the wings of the firebird. The fires on the hearthstones of all Moya's clan had been lit from the first fire brought by the great, rosy birds. If one's fire went out, he must light it from the hearth of another of his clan. But if the flamingoes were mistreated here where Ngai had hidden their nesting lake, the fires of all their clan would be extinguished, not to be kindled again, even by a fire stick from the sacred fig tree. Moreover, the spirits of their ancestors, who had taken the flamingo as a totem, would rise in wrath, sending sickness to the people and blight to their gardens.

Moya's eyes traveled about the blazing blue lake rimmed with the white shore and an inner rim of pink, from which a grating buzz arose, the voices of the flamingoes. Near the point where the stream ran into the lake, a knob of land jutted into the water, breaking the shoreline. Moya's sharp eyes discerned what looked like a flamingo garden. Moya could not count them, for counting brought misfortune to the thing counted. The flamingoes were packed closely together on the knob of land. Moya saw that some of the birds were sitting upon cylinders of mud, while others frantically flung mud into piles to make castle-like structures for themselves. It was a nesting colony!

Moya knew that there would be excitement in the village when they learned of it. He clambered up the ravines and cliffs, pulling himself up by the stout trunks of the leleshwa bushes. He ran breathless into his village.

"Kimani! Jolo!" he cried to his brothers. "The firebirds are nesting!"

"Let's go see them!" cried Jolo.

It had been remarked in the village that the firebirds had not nested on their lake for several seasons. The firebirds did not seem to observe the seasons as men did, performing certain jobs, in the season of the long rains, others in the season of the short rains, and some in the season of the big harvest. The flamingoes came and went according to no pattern.

"Another time, Jolo," Kimani frowned. "We have a job to do today. We're to sell the baskets that our mother and sisters and grandmothers have finished. Perhaps you can catch a glimpse of the lake as we go."

"But I have never seen their nests close," Jolo complained.

"It's better that way," Kimani told him. "Remember that the flamingoes are the totem of our clan, and we protect them. If you scare the flamingo off his nest, he will leave his eggs, and there'll be no new flamingoes."

"Bad luck will come to us," Moya added, wide-eyed and serious.

Kimani's eyes sharpened as he looked at Moya.

"What were you doing at the lake?" he asked. "It's your turn at bird scaring."

Moya had not remembered until then. A guilty look came over his face.

Kimani scowled at Moya.

"Can't I trust you to stay where you belong?" he demanded. "Wamboi, you may take the platform for today. I'll have to take this good-for-nothing along with me to sell baskets so that I can keep an eye on him. It's time he learned some responsibility."

Moya could not feel shame at being reprimanded, for the joy he felt at going with Kimani and the big boys was so much greater. He had always wished to go with them to sell baskets.

But he hid his joy and tried to look meek and sorrowful at Kimani's scolding.

2: *The Basket Merchants*

"Where are your baskets, Coco?" Kimani asked his grand-mother.

The old lady went into her conical thatched hut. Her skirt of delicate, beaded goatskin swung gracefully as she walked. She came out with an armful of baskets and mats.

"Ask a good price for them," she demanded, "for they are made of the finest fibres."

"Maito!" Kimani called to his mother, as they left their grandmother's hut and crossed to hers. "We've come for the baskets."

"Look in the store-room," she told them. The boys went into their mother's round hut, which was divided into wedge-shaped portions. They passed the room where a sheep was being fattened, past the fire, where charcoal glowed upon three flat stones, past their sister's compartment, where she was tending the baby, and then into the *thegi,* the store-room, where hands of green bananas hung from the center poles and piles of yams stood against the walls. The baskets made by their mother and sisters were heaped in a corner.

Moya slipped between his brothers and claimed one of the small gourd-shaped baskets he liked. Kimani distributed the others among the three of them.

"Is *Moya* going with you?" asked his sister, who had come to the compartment with the baby held on her hip. "Moya, that little round one is mine. It took me a long time to make it, and you had better sell it."

Moya nodded uncertainly. He feared he would not sell any at all, even when, as they started on their journey, he saw the flamingoes passing overhead bringing them luck.

In times past, things produced by the family would have been taken to the market and traded. Skins for milk, sugar cane for butter-fat, yams for jewelry, maize for digging sticks. But now, the family went as well to the road to Nakuru, where people came from all over the world to see the masses of flamingoes that shimmered on Lake Nakuru, and to hear the buzz of their voices and see them rise like huge pink umbrellas over the lake. The people liked the baskets that the women of the clan made. In those far-off countries, it must be that there were no baskets as beautiful as these.

When the boys reached the Rift Valley floor, Moya cried: "I'll race you to the top of that hill!"

The feet of Moya and his brothers flew along the plain towards a furrowed volcano. The baskets slapped the boys' arms as they raced.

Moya kept his lead until he reached the peak of the dead

volcano. Then the others saw him turn with a grimace of anger.

A shout came from the other side of the volcano: "Wakine!"

"Who's that?" Jolo scowled. "It sounds like that conceited Mobura."

"It is," Kimani said quietly. "Don't pick a fight with him. Keep your head."

Mobura, with his younger brothers, had reached the top of the crater and stood with Moya as Kimani and Jolo approached.

"So you have baskets to sell on the road to Nakuru!" Mobura jeered. "You'll sell them after we're through selling ours, for ours are of better quality, and will be bought first."

"If we're to see who will sell his baskets first, we must get moving. Flowing water waits for no one," Kimani said. He stood very straight, and looked without blinking into Mobura's face.

Kimani strode on across the plain, and the others followed, Mobura needling Moya and Jolo as they went. At last, Mobura grew tired of hearing himself talk and set off on a separate route with his companions.

When they had gone, Jolo complained to Kimani: "You always let Mobura get the better of you. Our baskets are brighter. They are woven more tightly. You have more to boast about, yet you have let him outdo you."

"If he outdoes me, then perhaps he's better fitted to be the *muthamaki*." The muthamaki was the leader of their age grade.

"What nonsense! Everyone knows you're the best of the leaders. Yet if all his bragging keeps up, he'll convince everyone that he is best."

"Does he convince you?"

"No, but..."

Kimani smiled and looked off into the distance, where a line of black-edged pink wings threaded its way against the cliffs.

"Maybe I don't want to be *muthamaki,* anyway," Kimani continued.

"But that's the best place in the age grade," Moya exclaimed. "Anyone would like to be *muthamaki.*"

"The age grade is not the whole world, Moya," Kimani said. "The age grade is a part of the clan, and the clan is a part of a tribe, and the tribe is a part of the country of Kenya. Have you seen how the people come from far away to see our firebirds and our animals? Yet there are some tribes who would do away with the animals to make more pasture land or land for gardens. More than a *muthamaki,* I would like to be a ranger, because our animals and birds are something special that must be cared for."

"Well, I would like to be leader of *my* age grade," Jolo said.

"I would like best to be a mondo-mogo. As a witch doctor, I would paint myself and wear feathers and masks and send away evil spirits and sickness," said Moya. Moya put his hands over his face and danced and chanted while the baskets bobbed up and down.

His brothers laughed. Moya had the words of the chant all

wrong. Moya a mondo-mogo! It was too funny to imagine!

Moya pouted at not being taken seriously.

The boys walked on toward the road, stopping only once to prod sticks into a bubbling, steaming spring that boiled from the side of a hillock.

"Does this really come from the cooking fires of people underground?" Moya asked, waving his hand toward the smoking geyser.

Kimani laughed. "That is what the legend says."

As the boys parted the gray-green shrubs that lined the edge of the road, they saw that Mobura and Bureki and Moruma had arrived there before them. They had joined hands and stretched themselves across the road so that a car had to stop. The driver was angry. He gestured to them to get out of the way.

Kimani did not like this way of doing business. He motioned to his brothers to follow him down the road to a clearing where they could display their baskets on the limbs of a tree. If drivers wished to stop and look, there was room for them to pull off the road.

As Kimani, Jolo and Moya passed on the other side of the road, they heard someone calling: "Hey, come over here. Let's see that big basket."

A boy with hair the color of millet was leaning out the back window of the station wagon Mobura and his brothers had stopped.

"Father, look," the blonde boy said. "This basket would be great for carrying my camera and binoculars around the lake. And one of those little ones would be a good present to take home to Sis."

The father turned from Mobura to Kimani, and sighed in resignation. "Okay. But pick them out quickly and let's get along."

"How much?" the boy asked Kimani.

"It is eight shillings," Kimani told him, separating the large basket made by his grandmother from the others, as Mobura looked on wrathfully.

"Are you going to see the flamingoes?" asked Kimani. He liked to practice his English. He had taught English to his smaller brothers, for he had been one of the few in his clan to go to school.

"Yes," said the boy eagerly. "My father is studying them. We hope to see the flamingoes on their nests. Is it the nesting season now?"

Kimani's eyes narrowed. "The flamingo does not know the seasons," he told the boy. He knew that no flamingoes nested upon Lake Nakuru, for the many visitors that came to the lake had long since frightened away the breeding colonies. Now, it was only upon such secret places as the Lake of the Firebirds, hidden and protected by their clan, that flamingoes would nest.

Moya thought of the river of scarlet that had poured this morning upon the lake, and of the garden of flamingoes with their ruffled-up feathers that now sat upon the sandbar, jostling, gabbling, spreading their wings, and snaking their long necks at one another as they vied for nesting places.

Moya wished the eager, bright-blue eyes of the boy could see that fantastic beauty, but like Kimani, he kept silent.

Mobura muscled in ahead of Moya again, cutting off his view of the car. Moya felt very small. He looked at the baskets on his arm. He would never sell them, because no one would ever see them.

The father, who had given his son enough shillings to buy Kimani's big basket was impatient to drive away. He was pushing the gas pedal, and the motor roared, warning the boys to get clear of the car.

"Wait, Dad, I have to get one for Sis. I saw one with a top on it and fringe around it. Where did that little guy go?" Peter searched among the boys and their baskets, until he found Moya, shoved behind the others. "You." His eyes fixed themselves on Moya's and seemed to draw him toward the car under the arms and baskets of the bigger boys. Moya ducked his head and pushed forward, gratitude bubbling up inside him.

"That one. That little bulgy basket with the fringe." Moya's heart soared as he lifted his sister's gay little basket from his arm.

The father impatiently doled out more shillings, revved his motor, and left the boys looking after him in the road.

Now, replacing the shining face of the foreign boy, Moya saw the angry eyes of Mobura looming over him.

"That was our car. We went to the trouble of stopping it," Mobura accused Kimani. "You had to interfere."

Kimani ignored him, and Mobura followed up the road quarrelling and picking on Moya and Jolo while they hung their baskets in a tree to display them to people traveling to Nakuru.

"Do you want to hang your baskets with ours, and we'll all see how many we can sell?" invited Kimani.

Mobura grudgingly agreed.

"Then let's be friendly. To work in a happy mood is to make the task easier." Kimani quoted a proverb of his clan.

When the shadows became long, many visitors had been attracted by the boys' bright baskets hung in the acacia tree, and all of the boys had many shillings to take home.

3: A Rescue

It had been two days since moya had seen the nesting colony. When the breeze was right, he could hear the voices of the flamingoes, and he had seen them, in increasing numbers, silhouetted against the sky or flaming in the sunset, pouring over from Nakuru and from the other lakes that dotted the Rift Valley.

Moya was eager for Kimani to go with him to see the nests. He waited while Kimani finished his work on his garden plot. He helped him dig sweet potatoes and pick beans and examine the ripening millet. Just as the work was finished, Wilau, their sister, begged Kimani:

"Help me clear this garden plot that father has given me. Just see all the rocks and that old tree stump! I'll never get it ready to plant before the time of long rains."

Moya turned away in disappointment as he saw that Kimani was going to help Wilau with a long, hard job. He would have to see the nests by himself, for Jolo and Wamboi were herding the goats and sheep.

Moya made his way down the rocky chasms and cliffs. He heard the buzz of the flamingo voices grow louder as he approached, swelling to a rhythmic roar as he reached the floor of the valley.

Moya always felt a shock of surprise when he saw the intense blue of the lake against the dazzling white of the shore and the varied roseate hues of the flamingo masses. His eyes strained towards the nesting colony for detail. He could make out frenzied flamingoes digging up mud with their beaks and plastering it onto their round heaps while others, probably the fathers, Moya thought, stood by with feathers erect like shaggy pom-pons.

Moya's glance moved back over the snowy shore. He had seen something along that shimmering crystal expanse. Something that did not belong there. A blot. A foreign object that did not move. Was it an animal, a gazelle or zebra which had come from the acacia thickets against the hills? Perhaps one of their own goats? Moya walked to the blinding whiteness of the lake shore. He picked his way along the dazzling crust of soda. Now and then his foot went through into the slimy, sour-smelling ooze below. Heat radiated in waves from the vast brilliance.

As Moya approached the blot on the stretch of white shore, he saw that it was a human being! It lay on its face, a bow and quiver of arrows strapped to its back. Moya thought his eyes must be playing tricks on him in this strange light. It couldn't be!

Lying beside the figure was his grandmother's basket, the one Kimani had sold the other day. Moya touched the basket to make sure it was real.

Moya knelt beside the figure, his knee cracking the soda crust. As he struggled to turn the face upward, crystals of

soda flew into the air, and Moya saw crystals clinging to the boy's clothes, and to the millet-colored hair. It was Peter, the boy from the road to Nakuru!

His face was red. Moya felt breath coming from his mouth. He saw his chest rising and falling. Moya himself felt dizzy with shock and the intense heat reflecting from the soda crystals.

Into his memory flashed the picture of a zebra that he and Kimani had once seen, dead on the soda shore of one of the lakes. It had sunk through the crust into the ooze, and there had died, parched to emptiness by the sun.

The same thing was sure to happen to Peter if he stayed where he was. Moya remembered his feeling of happiness when the boy had bought his basket.

He was very sick, Moya could tell. He needed a mondo-mogo. Yet, if Moya took the time to bring the mondo-mogo, it might be too late. Moya tugged at the boy. He could not move him. He tried rolling him. With effort, he could roll him from back to front, and then over. In this way, he would get him out of the sun.

The boy wore a tan shirt with short sleeves and short tan trousers. Moya took the bow and arrow off Peter's back and put it on his own. Placing his grandmother's basket that Peter had bought over his arm, he saw that it contained many heavy, complicated gadgets.

As Moya rolled Peter over and over across the rough crystals his sunburned skin became more and more irritated, so that Moya himself felt pain at each roll. Looking back, Moya saw the wide track, with the crust broken here and there where the boy's knees had gone through, or perhaps Moya's foot as he struggled to shove his heavy burden to safety. Back through the blur of white light, he saw the quivering pink of flamingoes in the heat waves, like a mirage.

As Moya rolled Peter farther, he noticed that the harsh crystals had worn away the skin of Peter's knees. He would need medicine for it.

At last, Moya reached a point where the soda crust thinned and gave way to firmer ground: hard packed earth to which a fuzz of downy pink flamingo feathers clung, with a few long pink quills discarded when the birds had molted. The sun still blazed mercilessly.

Moya's legs ached. The skin of his feet burned from the white hot soda crystals. The sharp, foul smell of the lake engulfed him.

The sun was at its zenith. Ordinarily, at this time of day, Moya would have been resting, perhaps sitting in the shade of the banana grove eating a juicy paw-paw, or maybe up in the breezy branches napping on his bird-scaring platform. No one was supposed to be out in the heat of the day. Even the animals: the leopards, the zebras, and the tender-skinned hippos, sought shelter from the sun in the heat of the day. All the animals did except the flamingoes, and nothing seemed to bother them. They continued their ceaseless buzzing out on the lake, and their constant search for food. Moya and his brothers had once seen flamingoes drinking from a stream of boiling water that ran from a geyser.

Moya became uneasy. If this boy from a strange country had collapsed in the heat, might not the same thing happen to him? His eyes searching for the nearest shade, he heard the boy moan. Afternoon clouds piled up in the sky. Moya shuddered with relief as a cloud passed over the sun and provided a temporary shade. He crouched beside his burden and examined him, swept by a sudden terror. The Lake of the Firebirds had never before been visited by a foreigner. He, Moya, one of the youngest of his clan, dared to rescue the first intruder who had ferreted out the secret lake. He remembered Peter's eager face in the car.

"We hope to see the flamingoes on their nests," he had said, and Kimani had frowned.

How had this boy known of the secret nesting place? He carried a bow and arrow. Had he meant to harm the fire-birds? Moya looked at him with fear and suspicion. He might cause the fires of their clan to go out.

Through Moya's mind passed the fearsome legends and tabus of their clan that his mother had sung him in lullabies, and his father and the older boys had taught him in stories and riddles. But as he looked at the helpless boy, and saw the cloud was moving off the sun, he felt fear of another kind, fear that he could not save Peter. Now that Moya had to care for him, he seemed to belong to Moya. No one had ever depended upon Moya before.

Moya knew that he must get the boy to the spring, and beyond that, to the cave, where he would be cool. When he awoke, Moya would explain to him that the flamingoes were his totem, and he would show him a safe route back to Nakuru, through a grove of trees and shrubbery.

Peter's knee was bleeding. Moya feared to roll him any more. He tugged at his feet, although it took all his strength. He could pull him only a few yards at a time. Then he would sit down, panting, to recover his breath before he could pull him farther.

The cloud passed off the sun. The blaze was reflected again from the lake shore. As Moya tugged Peter, he felt giddy and his knees buckled under him.

"We're both going to be lying here, senseless," he thought, "and no one ever comes this way. We will die."

A whirlwind wavered on the heat saturated plain.

"It's the evil spirits collecting, coming to kill me and my friend," Moya told himself. A flight of flamingoes set off from the lake and flew towards the plain, veering and banking and coming in at another point on the lake.

Moya sighed, and felt relief. The firebirds had frightened away the evil spirits, and the dust-devil had changed its course and disappeared into a haze of heat.

With a final burst of strength, Moya dragged his charge into the first scraggly shrubs near the stream, where the leaves and the spray from the spring made a little pocket of coolness.

Moya lay still a while, the sockets of his strained arm aching. After a while, he crawled to Peter. He was as big as Kimani. Moya got to his knees and crawled to the spring. Below, where the stream flowed into the lake, he saw flamingoes crowding to drink the fresh water, cleaning their beaks of the thick, foul liquid from the interior of the lake.

Moya cupped his hands, drinking from them. He filled them again, carrying the water to slosh in Peter's face. Most of it escaped through the cracks between his fingers as he walked. He wished he had a gourd for carrying water. Returning to the spring, he doused his burning feet, drank again, and carried more water in his hands. He tried to pour it in the boy's mouth, but most of it trickled down the sides of his face.

Refreshed, Moya dragged his friend the short distance through the shrubs to the cave. When he had him safely laid out on the cool rock floor, he looked back, panting with exhaustion. Those last few yards had been uphill. Moya could look out over the spring onto the lake through the screen of leleshwa bushes. He could faintly see the track over which he had dragged his friend. The flamingoes were a bright splotch in the turquoise of the lake.

4: Moya's Plan

THE NESTING COLONY STILL BUZZED WITH THE ACTIVITY ASSOCI-
ated with different stages of breeding. A breeze blowing over
the lake ruffled the feathers of birds that had been sitting for
some time on their nests; new arrivals, their great, plumy
bodies held aloft on pipestem legs, worked their shovel-like
beaks into the soupy mud, scooping it into piles, then stamp-
ing about their mud heaps with their black webbed feet to
make the mound symmetrical.

Moya's skin prickled with fear. With the slightest disturb-
ance, these birds could stampede into the sky, leaving their
nests barren, and misfortune would come to Moya's clan. Yet
he had brought a stranger here, a mysterious stranger whose
purpose Moya did not know.

Moya turned back to the cave. He looked unhappily at
Peter, whom he had rescued. The cave was cool. The angry
red of the boy's skin was fading slightly. It seemed to Moya
that he was breathing better, but parts of his legs and arms

were raw and sore where the crystals had torn his skin. One of his knees had swollen.

Moya crept to the spring for more water for his patient. Farther downstream, the flamingoes still gabbled impatiently for their turns to drink.

Moya had taken a square of cloth from the boy's basket and he dipped into the spring. Creeping back, he bathed Peter's hot face with it, and his arms and his legs. As he washed gently around the boy's torn and swollen knees, he could feel sharp soda crystals embedded in the edges of the wounds. Again, he returned to the stream, drenched the cloth and washed Peter's feverish body. The boy's skin seemed to grow paler as he cooled it.

When Moya had finished bathing his patient, he settled back to rest. He closed his eyes, which still burned from the glare of the lake shore. As his body relaxed, his troubles floated uppermost in his thoughts.

Moya suddenly felt very small. He did not know how he could have pulled this huge bulk of a boy so far. He wished for Kimani or his father. Yet, if they knew, they might find it necessary, for the good of the clan, to bring harm to Peter.

Moya looked at him again. Perhaps he was already under an evil spell. He needed the mondo-mogo. But the mondo-mogo would frown upon this stranger, with his weapons, at the Lake of the Firebirds.

Clearly, whatever help Peter got, he must get from Moya alone. His thoughts ranged through his whole experience, seeking a solution, until his memory focused upon something that would make everything right.

Moya would make Peter his blood brother! He would not be a stranger, but a member of the clan, bound by the clan laws to respect its totem, and one whom the clan would have to help.

But the boy would have to be conscious to be a blood brother. He must be doctored. He, Moya, would be the mondo-mogo.

In the excitement of his new plan, Moya's fatigue left him. His thoughts raced.

How was one made a blood brother? He had watched the older people do it, but he really did not remember what was to be done. He must find out quickly, before harm came to him, or to Peter, or to his village.

With fifteen minutes running, Moya could reach his village. He could find out how to make a person your blood brother. He could get food and medical supplies.

He would not need to leave Peter alone for long, and Peter would not know, anyway.

Moya stole from the cave quietly, so as not to disturb the flamingoes beside the stream, or those building their nests farther out. He hastened up the incline, past the terraced banana and vegetable patches of other households of his clan, and past their round, thatch-roofed, stilted houses, until he reached his own home.

Kimani was resting with some other boys of his age grade. Moya, breathless with his haste and secret plans, managed to get his attention.

"Kimani, how do two people become blood brothers?"

"Blood brothers! What questions you ask!"

"Most people," laughed one of the other boys, "have enough brothers of their own to answer to, without the trouble of a blood brother."

Moya persisted. "But if one *did* need a blood brother, how would he get one?"

The bigger boys laughed. "Little kids ask the craziest questions," one said.

"It's something done with coffee beans, isn't it?" said another.

"Yes, I remember hearing a story of it," Kimani said. "Each of the people has a coffee berry, and he opens it and there are two beans in it. Then each person cuts himself, puts his bean in the blood, eats one half, and gives the other to his blood brother to eat."

"Oh, yes, I know," said another boy. "Those beans just stay inside you and keep you loyal as brothers. If you're not loyal, the beans will swell up and kill you."

"After they swallow the beans, they put their weapons behind them, to show they'll never fight. Then they have a big feast," Kimani concluded.

"And that's all?" Moya asked, crouching at his feet.

"Yes, I guess so," Kimani laughed. As Moya rushed into the hut, he smiled at his friends: "The little boys must be playing a game."

5: The Witch Doctor's Hut

MOYA'S MOTHER WAS INSIDE THE HOUSE MAKING MILLET CAKES.

"You look tired, Moya. Have you been running about in the heat of the day?"

"I'm not tired, Maito, only hungry."

His mother gave him a millet cake.

"I was looking for some coffee berries," he told her. "Do you have any?"

"Coffee berries! None at all. They are only ripening now," she told him.

Moya found a couple of calabashes in the store room. He filled one with milk, and took some bananas and yams in a basket. He needed a weapon. One of his mother's cooking knives would do.

Moya hoped that his mother would not notice him as he went out with the supplies. Her back was towards him as she shaped the millet cakes over three hot stones of the hearth.

"Do not get overheated, Moya," she said, without looking up.

"No, Maito," Moya said. Looking at the glowing charcoal between the stones where his mother worked, it occurred to him that he would have to have a coal of fire to take back to the cave, for they would need a fire both for the ceremonies of the mondo-mogo and for cooking and protecting themselves from animals.

Taking a coal would arouse his mother's suspicions. And how would he carry it? He stepped back into the store-room. A small clay jar would make a good vessel for carrying fire. Moya peeked out the store-room door. His mother had finished the millet cakes.

"I'm taking these to Coco," she told Moya.

What luck! Moya scurried to the hearth and chose a large, glowing coal, placing it carefully in the pot.

Moya took stock of his supplies: he had fire, food, milk, a calabash for carrying water, a weapon for the blood brother ceremony. He still needed medical supplies and coffee beans.

As he hurried out his mother's door, bound for the coffee grove of a neighbor higher up the hill, a boy of his age grade called to him: "Moya, Moya, where have you been? We've been looking for you to play on our hoop-spearing team." He ran alongside Moya as he spoke.

"Not now," Moya said impatiently, brushing him aside. "I have a job to do." He outdistanced the boy, so that he did not hear him calling after him: "Moya, did you hear that an officer of the Game Department was here asking if anyone has heard of an American boy who is lost?"

His words were lost in the breeze, for Moya streaked toward the banana grove. A mondo-mogo needed banana leaves for holding water and for sweeping.

He hacked off the thick banana leaves toward the base with his mother's cooking knife, and ran on toward his neighbor's coffee farm. The coffee berries were not ripe, but that did not matter. Green ones could be swallowed as well as ripe ones.

Moya ran from the coffee farm to the house of the mondo-mogo. He saw the witch doctor leaving his hut.

"Wait! Wait!" Moya called. "I need medicine."

Moya noticed that the witch doctor did not have on his ceremonial dress. His body was not painted, and he was not carrying his masks and other equipment.

"Yes, Moya." The mondo-mogo smiled pleasantly, but Moya saw impatience under his smile, as though he were in a hurry.

"I wanted to know," Moya asked him, "if someone has cut himself on the soda crystals by the lake, and the cut is swelling, is there medicine for this?"

"You must be more careful, Moya," said the mondo-mogo, as if he were thinking of something else. "Yes, there is an ointment of herbs. Look in the gourd that is painted with ochre, and which has three black stripes. When you have smeared ointment on, you must cover it with one of the leaves which are near the gourd."

The mondo-mogo was Moya's friend, and often let him visit in his hut. He had showed him the things in his magical bag of monkey-skin, and the other pieces of equipment he kept in his hut. Best of all, Moya liked to hear him ring the *rogambi,* the magic bell. Moya knew where the ochre-colored gourd with the three black stripes was.

As he entered the mondo-mogo's hut, he pictured himself in mask and feathers, painted fantastically like the medicine man. He had often thought of himself as the mondo-mogo of his clan. And now he would be mondo-mogo sooner than he had imagined.

Moya looked into the calabash of ointment. Beside it were leaves of a sort the mondo-mogo used to place over cuts and wounds. Moya took some of the ointment, wrapped it in a covering of leaves, and looked about the hut. It was creepy to be there without the mondo-mogo. The masks stared empty-eyed at him, their teeth bared in fierce grins or scowls. Some were topped with feathers. One wore a crown of flamingo quills. He saw the paints which the witch doctor used to decorate his body for a ceremony. Did Moya dare? If he painted himself, the boys might see him going through the village, and they would be suspicious. Yet, if Moya was to be a proper mondo-mogo, he must be painted.

Moya stood hesitantly before the paint pots. Then, quickly jabbing first one finger, then another, into the pots, he decorated both sides of his body with vari-colored stripes.

He tried to remember the actions of the mondo-mogo when he had cured his small sister, and also his grandfather. The gazelle's horn, filled with white powder had been an important part of the ceremony. The *rogambi* was necessary. And the mask with the radiant flamingo quills. Moya knew he could cure Peter with that. One by one, the medicine man's equipment went into the basket. At the door of the mondo-mogo's hut, Moya looked out cautiously.

The boys who were getting up the hoop-spearing team were nowhere in sight. Kimani and his friends were off to one side of the cluster of houses. Their backs were toward Moya. There was no one else around, unless Moya's mother should suddenly come out of his grandmother's hut. The coast was clear.

Gleaming in his rainbow paint, Moya made his way across the clearing of the huts of their household, and disappeared into a grove of trees. He stopped only once in his flight back to the Lake of the Firebirds, to gather some fruit from a paw-paw tree.

Taking a long, forked stick, he loosened the lowest fruit on the knobbly trunk. It was bright yellow, and hung, heavy with juice, on the umbrella-like tree. He shoved at the paw-paw until it came loose and plopped to the ground. Then he sat and ate the paw-paw, scooping out the round, gooey black seeds in the center and devouring the sweet, juicy flesh

around them. A pleasant perfume-like aroma came from the fruit.

When he had plucked more paw-paws for his basket, he set off again toward the cave, and going farther and farther from his home, he felt more and more like a real mondo-mogo.

6: Caught

Moya became weary on the journey back to the cave. His bare feet hurt from clambering over the rocks with his heavy burden of medical supplies and food. Now and again he looked into the clay pot in the basket to see if the coal of fire was still alive.

He worried about his patient as he walked, hoping Peter had not awakened, for he wanted to be there when he did. And what if Peter had awakened and had gone away! Moya hurried. He did not want to lose the chance to be a mondo-mogo. He took the *rogambi,* the magic bell, from the basket and listened to it. He planned to do a dance around his patient as he had seen the witch doctor do.

It was the end of the afternoon. The heat that had collected all day in the Rift Valley rose up the cliffs like a suffocating blanket. The rocks and ravines over which Moya traveled were so hot he felt his feet blistering. He wondered if he would have to use the mondo-mogo's salve on himself before he reached his patient.

His throat felt dry. He wished he were near the spring as now and again he sat down to rest, and listened for the conversation of the flamingoes down on the lake. Whiffs of the lake's acrid odor rose through the heat waves.

Moya heard a human sound rise above the flamingoes' voices. It was his patient awake.

Moya plunged down the short way that remained between him and the cave. As he ran, he dislodged rocks here and there. They crashed and echoed down the cliff, rustling the bushes, and then their sound was lost in the buzz of the flamingoes.

Moya heard the cry again. He could hear the boy shouting, "Help!"

He forgot his caution and lurched ahead without looking. As he ran, his foot slipped into a crack in the cliff. Just at that moment, a fragment of rock crashed past him, narrowly missing his head, and lodged itself above Moya's foot in the crack.

Moya's ankle had twisted and he felt sharp pain. He turned his leg to dislodge his foot, but it was stuck fast, and the rock in the crevice had wedged it in.

Moya put down his basket of supplies. He looked about him for a stick strong enough to shake loose the tightly lodged rock. There was none. He tried to stretch his body to reach the shrubs around him. He could just reach the end of a branch, but he could not tear it off. In trying, he only pulled leaves off the end of the branch, and then the tip of it, so that it snapped back and he could no longer reach it.

He bent over and explored the crevice with his hand, pushing and shoving at the rock, but it would not come free. The cry for help sounded from the cave again.

"I'm coming," Moya called.

He did not hear the cry again for a few minutes.

Moya tugged and pulled at the rock. He looked anxiously into his clay pot to see whether the coal of fire had gone out. It still glowed, though the glow was shrinking farther into the center.

"Help!" the voice shouted again.

"I'm coming," Moya answered. But he was not certain that he could. The sun sank beyond the opposite escarpment of the Rift Valley and the shadows became purple. Moya saw a line of flamingoes pass above the cliffs. They were scarlet in the setting sun. The sun sank quickly, and darkness deepened. Moya was not afraid for himself, but for the boy in the cave, he shuddered. The boy needed a friend and a fire.

He shouted to him: "I am coming. My foot is caught." He was glad that Kimani had taught him English.

"Where are you?" the voice called.

"Nearby. I bring fire!" shouted Moya.

"I am hurt. I am sick. I need help!" the boy shouted.

"I know. I bring help," Moya said uncertainly. He looked into the clay pot. The glow of the coal had become smaller. Moya found a chip of wood that might take fire from the coal. He dropped it in the fire pot.

Moya picked up a rock and banged it on the first one. All

the light was gone from the sky. The heat from the valley was escaping upwards, and was leaving the rocks, also.

"Who are you?" the voice of Peter came through the night.

"I am Moya, the witch doctor. I am coming to make you well."

The boy's voice did not answer.

Moya's foot ached and cramped from the cold, and from being in one position so long. He shifted it a fraction in the crevice, and as he did, he felt the wedged rock move. The cold of the night had made the rock contract. Moya moved his hand again into the crack, breaking the rock loose. He brought it up with a shout of joy.

"I'm free!" he yelled happily, picking up his basket. The coal had lighted the wood chip, starting a new fire. He felt his way carefully down the rocks, making sure that he did not slip again. His ankle throbbed from the twisting, but he was too busy to think about it. As Moya slipped down toward the cave, he saw the ghostly, glowing forms of the flamingoes downstream drinking the spring water.

7: The Cure

Moya could barely see the boy with the light of the moon, which was rising in the sky.

The boy sat halfway up, the pain on his face turning to astonishment as he saw the weirdly painted boy silhouetted in the entrance to the cave.

"You're only a kid," he said. He seemed relieved. "I thought you said you were a witch doctor."

"Yes," said Moya. "I must be the medicine man for you, so that others may not see you in this forbidden place."

"Forbidden?"

"The Lake of the Firebird," Moya said.

"Firebirds? Oh, you mean flamingoes. I remember. I was walking along the shore to see them, and suddenly I felt dizzy. But where am I now? How did I get here?"

"I brought you in from the sun," Moya answered. "You bought my basket. This is my brother's cave."

"Your basket! Are you *that* kid? The *little* one? You brought me here?"

"It was hard," Moya acknowledged.

Moya laid out one of his banana leaves upon the stone floor of the cave, so that it had a depression in the center.

"I must get water," Moya said.

"Water. Yes, that is what I need," Peter said.

Moya ran to the spring with his calabash and filled it with water. He gave some to Peter to drink, then poured the rest in the banana leaf, ringing the *rogambi* above it. Then he removed the top from the powder horn.

"You must lick the powder and then spit it into the water in the leaf," he told Peter.

Peter dimly saw Moya hold out the horn.

"Not me," he exclaimed. "It looks like poison."

It was not in Moya's plan that his patient might refuse.

"Gosh!" Peter exclaimed. "I have to get out of here. This leg of mine is paining so bad I can't move it. You have to get my father!"

"After you are well," Moya told him. "After you are my blood brother."

"This is crazy," the bigger boy said. "Something is really wrong with my legs, and my dad will be frantic. It's no time to play games."

"This will make your legs well," Moya pleaded. "Do what I say. This is not poison. It is *gethiito,* the powder that makes one well. Lick it. Spit it into the leaf. The evil spirits that make you sick will come out of you."

"No, thanks," said Peter. "I want my dad."

A great tear came to Moya's eye. He was going to fail in his first try at being a mondo-mogo.

"See, it's not poison. I, myself, will eat some." Moya put some on his tongue, and spit it out. "That is all you do," he begged.

The bigger boy suddenly looked amused. Moya was so small.

"Well, I'll go along with a gag," he decided. He leaned forward to lick some powder from the horn, and as he leaned, his face contorted with the pain of his blisters and of his infected and swollen legs. He licked the powder and spit it into the leaf.

"Could I have some more water?" he asked.

Moya filled the calabash again. Peter drank a long draught, while Moya rang the *rogambi*. That was the part of the healing ceremony he liked best.

"Now I will fix your sores." Moya took the ointment from the leaves.

"What's that? More poison?" Peter asked.

"It is herbs from the mondo-mogo, the medicine man," Moya said.

"Well, I guess if I'm going to die, I'm going to die," Peter said.

"You will be well," Moya told him positively.

He spread the ointment over the places where he could remember that Peter's skin was broken, though he could not see well in the shadowy cave. He covered the ointment with the leaves, as the mondo-mogo had told him.

"This will draw the evil spirits from your body," Moya

told him. "Now I must send them all away from this cave." He looked in the clay pot to see that his fire still glowed.

Moya put on the mask with the flamingo quills, and then grasped the banana leaf by its thick stem and swept the cave. He swept all the dust into a pile at the front of the cave. As he swept, he danced and chanted, though he could not remember all the words the mondo-mogo used. He knew it was something about sweeping away the evil spirits. He rang the magic bell at the mouth of the cave. Then he picked up the dust heap he had swept and put it in the water of the leaf.

"This is really spooky," his patient said.

"Evil spirits, I drown you," Moya addressed the banana leaf. Then he dusted the sick boy's body with another banana leaf in case any spirits were clinging to him.

He buried the leaf and all the evil spirits in it under the ground. He should have thrown it in deep water, but he was afraid of harming the flamingoes.

"That's some routine," the boy remarked. "But I still can't move. I need my dad."

"It takes time," Moya said, happy that he had successfully performed as a mondo-mogo. Now, the only tasks left were to build the fire, and then to make Peter his blood brother.

As he groped through the cave to feel out three flat stones for their fireplace, he looked uneasily at the shadowy figure of his patient, wondering if he would consent to be a blood brother. He might not cooperate.

Moya laid out the three stones, and then selected some twigs and dry grasses from the mouth of the cave. The coal

was almost out when Moya placed it on the dry grasses, but the grasses flared and the sticks crackled. An aromatic smell came from the branches. Moya found larger twigs and branches just outside the cave, and he made a store of them so that he could keep the fire burning.

"This is cozy," said Peter as the firelight leaped into the dark corners of the cave and flickered on the ceiling. He saw the long shadow of Moya and his feather headdress. "But frankly, that mask gives me the willies. How long do you have to wear it?"

"That's enough." Moya took off the mask, for it was so heavy it was hurting him. He set it up in the corner, where it still grinned eerily at the boys.

"You know," said Peter. "Maybe you do have something. My legs are beginning to feel better. That stuff is cool. My skin was really hot before."

"You might have died by the Lake of the Firebirds," Moya said.

"I remember how I got here." Peter sat up on his elbow. "My dad is crazy to see some flamingoes on nests. He teaches ornithology back at the college, and he's read about how the colonies of flamingoes over here in Africa are the greatest sight in the world, so we came here and no one seems to know just when or where you can see the flamingo nests. Dad saw these courtship dances on Lake Nakuru, and he said, 'The flamingoes are going to nest soon.' Someone said, 'not on Nakuru. They used to nest here, but too many people came, and they won't nest here any more!'

"So Dad went off to get supplies, and I saw these courting

flamingoes taking off, and I followed them so I could tell Dad where their nests are. I walked for hours, and finally konked out at this lake where I thought they were landing."

Moya did not understand all of Peter's speech, but he liked to hear him talking of the flamingoes.

"You will be in danger if anyone finds out you are here," Moya told him. "The flamingo is the totem of our clan. We protect its nesting place from strangers."

The fire glowed and the pleasant smell of smoke and the sounds from thousands of flamingoes floated into the cave as the boy talked.

"In danger? Are they going to boil me in a pot like in the movies?" Peter asked.

Moya looked puzzled. "They might put an evil spirit upon you so you would not get well," he said.

Peter was silent.

"If you are my blood brother," Moya continued, "you will not be in danger. You can see the nests safely. You will be a member of the clan. The flamingo will be your totem, also, and you will be their protector."

"How do I get into the clan?"

"It's easy," Moya said, relieved that Peter was receptive.

"Before we get mixed up in that," Peter said, eyeing the mask uneasily, "do you have anything to eat? I'm famished."

Moya brought out the calabash of milk and a banana.

Peter ate hungrily.

8: *The Magic Bell*

MOYA PUT MORE STICKS ON THE FIRE AND CREPT BACK INTO THE cave where he had placed the coffee beans and food for their brotherhood feast.

Peter turned restlessly from side to side on the hard rock floor of the cave while Moya brought the coffee beans and his knife. He got Peter's bow and arrow.

"To become blood brothers," he began to explain to Peter, "I will first cut myself so that blood will come out."

Peter tossed again.

"Please, no more ceremonies, medicine man." His smile had pain in it, which Moya could see in the flickering firelight that gave his face a reddish cast. Grotesque shadows played over Peter's features.

The hurt on Peter's face made Moya sad. He put the coffee beans away until tomorrow. He slipped out of the cave on the side where he had seen an acacia tree growing. The acacias had delicate leaves on small, soft stems. They made a nice bed. He cracked off a number of boughs, arranging a bed of soft leaves for Peter.

"Now you will be more comfortable," he told Peter.

Peter gritted his teeth tightly together as he eased himself onto the leaf bed, and Moya pressed the leaves around him.

"They are cool," he whispered. Moya busily arranged them and gathered more boughs to make a pillow. "I wish I had a sheepskin from my mother's house for you," he said. "Tomorrow I will get one."

"Tomorrow we must find my father," muttered Peter. "He must be worried."

Moya thought of his own father. Would he know he was gone? Sometimes he or his brothers slept in the tree on the birdscaring platform. There were two huts for boys, and if he was not in one, they would think he was in the other. But he was too tired to worry. He had pulled Peter here and had been back and forth to the village and worked as a mondo-mogo. It had been the hardest day of his life. He longed to sleep.

"Water," Peter said drowsily. Moya reached into the shadows of the cave for the calabash. It was empty again.

Moya started for the spring. He took the brass *rogambi* with him. Its strange tinkle kept him company and seemed to protect him on the way to the spring.

The murmur of flamingoes was louder. Moya saw that their number had increased. He watched for a moment as they swam and drank the fresh water. He saw one flap its wide wings, pale and ghostlike in the moonlight, and the others started away and then came back to their drinking again. Those swimming jostled the drinkers for a turn. Moya liked to watch them.

He pushed his calabash into the water, and as he did, the *rogambi* fell from his other hand, its magical sound lost in the gurgling of the spring. There was a deep pool here, hollowed out of the rock by centuries of running water. Moya set aside his calabash and rummaged on the bottom of the pool for his bell. He could not find it. A knot of fear twisted in his diaphragm. The *rogambi* was a part of the mondo-mogo's magic. He could not work without it. Early in the morning, when the first light came, Moya must find the *rogambi* in the pool, and he must carry it straight to the mondo-mogo with the healing horn and the mask of flamingo quills.

Moya trudged back into the cave. He placed a few of the stoutest sticks on the stones, for the fire must last the night. He knew he was going to sleep immediately. Before he did, he took Peter's cloth, and with some cool water from the calabash, he washed Peter's hands and arms again.

"Thanks," Peter said. Moya could barely see his eyes gleaming under their lids.

"I must rest," Moya said, "but the fire must not go out. If you are awake, shout at me, so I can keep the fire alive."

"Okay," Peter said, as if from far away. "Thanks for helping me."

Moya smiled. Peter was a good friend. Then Moya's eyes would not stay open any longer. He went to sleep, lulled by the buzzing and cries of the masses of flamingoes on the lake below.

9: The Flamingo Dance

IN THE MORNING, WHEN MOYA WOKE, CHARCOAL STILL GLOWED on the hearthstones. Peter sat up against the cave wall.

"Gee, my legs are better. See how the swelling has gone down. You're a good witch doctor."

The thought of the *rogambi* sprang to Moya's mind and brought a shadow of uneasiness.

"Now I can really see you," Peter said. "You're even smaller than I thought. I can't figure out how you got me up here."

"I have a brother your size," said Moya, as if in defense of his smallness. Most of the paint had worn off Moya's body as he slept, but it still clung in shreds to the side of his body.

"Moya, there are two things I need today," Peter told him. Moya liked Peter's eyes, clear like Kimani's. They looked straight at you. They were the color of the sky.

"What is that?"

"Well, first, I'm starved. Do you think you could find me

some food? And after that, could you find my father? He was going to stay at the White Stag Hotel in Nakuru."

Moya smiled widely. "I have food." He produced bananas and yams from the back of the cave, took out his knife, and started to peel a yam. The milk had soured and congealed in the gourd. He handed Peter half a peeled, raw yam. Peter gulped. He was used to cooked ones.

"I think I'll start with a banana," he said.

The angry red color that Moya had seen on Peter's skin had gone away. The ointment and the leaves with which he had made a poultice had drawn the soreness from his legs, where they had been infected by the soda crystals and the dirt on the lake shore. He could move his legs much better, and he could stand and walk.

"You're a good doctor," he said again as he stood up. Moya smiled proudly and looked over at the fantastic flamingo mask, remembering.

"I am going to be the mondo-mogo of my clan when I grow up," Moya told him, crunching a yam. The smell of banana filled the cave as Peter peeled his second fruit. He watched Moya eating the yam.

"I never ate one of those raw. How do they taste?" he asked.

"Try one," Moya said. "I'll cook some, besides."

He wrapped a couple of yams in leaves and set them on the hot rocks. He threw some more sticks on the fire.

"Have some milk," Moya passed the gourd to Peter.

"Ick, it's sour. Thanks anyway."

Moya drank the sour milk himself. He liked it that way.

As the yams heated, they spread their sweet, pungent aroma through the cave. Peter devoured another banana.

"I'll look for your father after I have been to the village," Moya told him. "I have to take back the witch doctor's magic: his *gethiito,* which is making you well, and his mask and *rogambi.*" A frown crossed Moya's face. He must go now to find the bell.

Moya took the calabash to the spring to fill it as he searched. But in the clear water in the hollow below the spring, there was no bell. He searched in the shrubbery beside the pool. He did not find it.

He stayed so long searching for the *rogambi* that Peter called to him.

Moya stumbled back to the cave, downcast.

"The *rogambi* is gone," he told Peter.

"What's that?"

"The magic bell of the mondo-mogo. He needs it whenever he heals a person. It is not like other bells. It was given to him by his father, and so on, back to the age grade of the Agu na Agu, and that is as far back as time goes. I borrowed it from him to heal you, and I did not tell him I had borrowed it."

"I'll help you look," Peter said. "After all, it's my fault you had it. Where do you think it is?"

"I heard it drop into the pool last night. But I couldn't see it."

"Where's this spring?" Peter asked, looking out of the cave.

Moya waved toward it. "But it's no use. I've searched."

"I want to help. I need to move around, because my muscles are cramped. You can't imagine how much better I feel than I did last night. Come on. Let's find that bell." Peter limped from the cave as he spoke. He walked slowly through the shrubs that screened the cave.

When Peter came within full sight of the lake, he whistled. His eyes grew large with wonder at the expanse of birds, which stretched in a field of pink almost to the center of the lake. His eyes swept over it to the nesting promontory, where thousands of pale pink bodies sat upon their eggs, while hundreds more still crowded in to build their little mud castles and lay their eggs.

"Wow! I've got to get Dad!" he exclaimed. "This is what he came to Africa to see!"

"Shhh," Moya frowned. "We have to be still when the birds are on their nests." He remembered that Peter was still an outsider, the first who had ever looked upon the Lake of the Firebirds. Moya's insides turned to jelly as his troubles swelled and filled his mind. He had the *gethiito,* the *rogambi* was lost, and he was profaning the sacred place of his clan. He should not have delayed making Peter a blood brother. After they found the bell, he would do it immediately. If he did not find the bell, then it was no use to go back. He would be shunned by his age grade.

Moya's gloomy face contrasted with Peter's joyous one as he exulted in the fantastic garden of color, movement and sound below him.

Peter struck his head in wonder.

"Everything is here! Look. A display has begun!" Peter

pointed to a group of flamingoes down on the shore that were brighter in color than the others. "See, they set their feathers in a special way, so that the prisms in them will catch the light to make them red!" Peter said. The flamingoes were dancing with a curious, jerky movement.

"We can't disturb them," Moya said nervously. "For the nests will be left, and the chicks will not hatch."

"We'll have to make a hide out so we can watch them!" Peter whispered and shouted at the same time. "We'll get a lot of branches and make ourselves a blind."

Peter seemed to have forgotten his wounds. He limped rapidly back to the cave.

"Come on. Carry some branches."

There was a crackling of wood and the pungent odor of sap as Peter filled his arms with large branches.

"Come on, Moya. We'll hold them in front of us and move slowly down the lake shore until we get close. They'll never know we're there."

Moya uncertainly broke off a few branches. Peter wove the twigs of them loosely together until they formed a portable screen, and then he made one for Moya. With the screen in front of him, he began moving away from the spring, down the creek where the flamingoes were drinking. Moving after him, Moya felt bewildered and frightened. The two boys looked like leleshwa shrubs being moved by the breeze. They reached a point along the fresh water stream just above the place where it flowed into the lake.

"I'm stopping to rest," Peter whispered. The boys sat down with their screens over them.

"Look at that!" Peter whispered, pointing to the group of dancing, deep rose flamingoes that stood out among the pink.

The group of birds had packed themselves closely together, and they hurried through the shallow water, calling in excitement and pushing aside other flamingoes. As they rammed through throngs of feeding flamingoes, some of the others would join them, as snowflakes join a snowball, and they would add their voices to the excited chorus, snapping their necks back and forth, looking up, then down. Some of the birds at the edge of the great rose-colored snowball spread their necks up to the greatest height, their beaks held heavenward, stretching their wings straight out to display their six-foot span. Then they snapped their wings closed, and brought down their necks like jack knife blades.

Peter whispered excitedly from beneath his screen of boughs. "I wish I had my camera here so I could show this to Dad."

10: A Forest of Firebirds

OVER THE ROAR OF THE FLAMINGOES ON THE LAKE AND THE higher pitched cries of the hundreds of flamingoes in the mating dance, Moya heard a disturbing rustling of leaves and a murmur of human voices. Moya touched Peter and whispered: "Someone is coming. They must not see us."

Peter and Moya lay very still under their canopies of branches.

"He doesn't seem to be around the lake," he heard the scornful voice of Mobura. Out of the corner of his eye, he saw Mobura's brothers, Bureki and Moruma. Mobura scanned the lake, seemingly unimpressed by the dancing flamingoes.

"Let's get a drink and go back," one brother said.

"Yes, nobody would come here, even if he was running away with the mondo-mogo's magic."

Moya stiffened. They were looking for him! The mondo-mogo already had discovered his things were gone. He was in trouble.

"Let's hurry back. Somebody has got to find him before the old man gets any sicker."

Moya heard the gurgling of the water as they drank. Then they got up to go.

"Do you smell smoke?" one of the boys asked. "And something like yams cooking?"

Moya almost stopped breathing. They would discover the cave with his fire and the *gethiito* and the bow and arrow and his basket of possessions. They would take him back to the village in disgrace.

Mobura sniffed. "I don't smell anything. Well, maybe there's a Tugen herdsman burning grass over in the valley. Come on. Let's go." The boys walked downstream, toward the drinking birds.

An icicle of fear froze Moya's heart. A few steps further, and they would discover him. Some of the drinking birds ran along the creek, splatting their black feet on the mud, and rose flapping and crying into the air at the boys' approach, but others remained on the ground.

"See how close to the birds we have come, Mobura, and they have not flown away."

"Ha! They cannot fly because they have to run first and we are in their path," said Mobura, important with his knowledge. "See, I'll show you that they can't fly."

"But, Mobura, don't. The fires may go out in the village," said Bureki, his voice trembling.

"Pooh, that's just a legend," Mobura scoffed.

Moya gasped at his boldness. He had picked up a stick and he was going to prod a flamingo with it. The flamingoes had pushed themselves together until they looked like a tremendous pink monster with dozens of legs and many heads emerging from its body, their hooked beaks all pointing toward Mobura and his brothers.

Suddenly a series of harsh honks sounded. Scores of huge black-edged wings rose from the mass of feathers and flapped wildly, wings beating upon wings, and the forest of long, spindly black legs began to move as one.

Moya put his hands up beside his face like blinkers, and then laced his fingers over his eyes so he was only looking through a little crack of light.

He saw Mobura fling up his arms, turn and run. Another boy scurried off. The flamingoes had lowered their heads, extended their long necks straight ahead of them. They drove ahead, thrusting their curved beaks like scimitars toward the enemy.

Moya almost cried out. The third boy had been overtaken by the flamingoes, knocked down, and their big feet flapped over him as they sloshed past the stream and over the shore. The great pink herd churned about and ran back across the stream.

Moya noticed that the gabbling of the flamingoes over the entire lake had stopped. He heard a rush of air. The sky was pink with flamingoes, and their voices echoed and re-echoed from the lake. Even the flamingoes from the nesting colony started off their nests, and trampling the carefully built mounds, raced across the mudflat and took wing.

Moya looked in dismay to see a large white egg roll from one of the nests, and he saw it crushed by the feet of stampeding flamingoes. His eyes darted back to the boy on the ground, who stirred, pushed himself up on hands and knees, rocked back and forth a moment, then stood unsteadily and limped off.

Moya watched with troubled eyes as the birds wheeled, disturbed, in the sky. Peter was mute with surprise in his blind.

It had been many seasons since a colony had completed its nesting. The good fortune that nesting birds brought to their clan had turned to bad. If Moya were caught here now with a stranger and the fresh nests abandoned, he would be blamed.

"There's no use being quiet any more. Everything is ruined," said Peter, emerging from his blind. "What was that all about?"

"They spoke in my language," Moya answered. He repeated the conversation, and told Peter that Mobura was the rival of his brother, Kimani, and wished to bring dishonor to him.

"Everyone must be searching for me. Someone is sick in the village, and he cannot be cured because I have the *gethi-ito* and the *rogambi*. If I do not find the bell, he might die."

"I had forgotten about the bell," Peter confessed. He looked upward in awe at the great, milling cloud of flamingoes and heard their discontented voices.

"Now they will leave our lake. Our clan will have bad luck," Moya added disconsolately.

"Wait! They aren't flying away. Get down again." Peter slipped under the branches of his blind, and Moya crawled under his. The lake and its surroundings looked peaceful again. A flock of young, grayish birds which had not yet acquired their pink feathers, stood sieving mud in the lake. The airborne flamingoes wheeled over the nesting ground. They circled lower and lower until they approached the ground. Large black feet and sticklike legs settled gently upon the sandbar. The birds strode among the nest-heaps and eggs, quarrelling and prodding one another. Moya stored up the scene in his mind, for he planned to tell Kimani about it. He would tell him how he wondered at each flamingo finding its own nest from the masses of them crowded close together on the sandbar.

Where eggs had been trampled in the helter-skelter departure, Moya wondered if the flamingoes would lay more eggs.

Some of the birds set to rebuilding their ruined nests, while the flamingoes that were not nesting landed in the shallows, hopping and dancing about, shaking their necks as they stirred up mud, their bodies circling around and around.

"I did not think the flamingoes would return," Moya whispered to Peter.

"I guess my Dad is right. He says no one has ever been able to predict what a flamingo will do next. But I think I know why they came back. While they were gone, I could see some little fuzzy gray chicks that had already hatched. I have heard that the flamingoes will abandon their eggs, but not their new-born chicks. Not till they're about two weeks old, anyway, and can go off on their own."

Moya's joy that the birds had returned faded again into fear, as he thought of the missing *rogambi.*

Peter inched down the stream bank in his blind until he was only a few feet from the flamingoes. The birds towered six feet above him. Peter came so close that when they snaked their long necks into the water to drink, he could see the structure of their beaks, the lower part being thicker and curved upward, the upper part shallow, curved over the lower like a clamshell. He could even see the little hairs on the edge, and the strainers on the insides of their beaks.

Down the stream at the lake edge, flamingoes sat in the fresh water bathing, preening, splashing and shaking their feathers. There was a hum of bird voices.

Peter looked closely again at the flamingo beaks drinking water. He stared, and started forward. He had seen a foreign glint in the water.

"Moya. Psst! come here."

Moya shuffled himself and his shell of branches to Peter's side.

"In there, by that big fellow's beak, I thought I saw something brass." Peter's whisper was almost drowned out by the rasping voices of the flamingoes.

Moya looked, but the big flamingo was pushed aside by others impatient to get their turns at the drinking place.

Their black-webbed feet and hooked beaks stirred up the water. Peter looked sharply. "There!" he whispered. "Quick. His beak is up. Look before he gets it down."

Through the swirling water, Moya saw the metallic gleam. He focussed his eyes with great concentration, and discerned a bit of curious carving upon pale metal. It was the *rogambi!* It had drifted downstream and now might be trampled by the feet of the flamingoes, pushed by their beaks farther down the stream to the bathing place and at last would be shoved down under the foul mud of the lake itself, never to be seen again.

Moya's thoughts flashed to the kind mondo-mogo, who was now desperate for his bell, to the villagers who searched for him and the *gethiito,* and to the sick man.

The gleam of the bell disappeared again in a swirl of water.

Moya's eyes traveled up the long legs of the flamingoes to their pink-plumed bodies. He could see the delicate structure of their feathers. He slithered on his stomach, the branches over him moving smoothly, so slowly that the motion could not be noticed. He moved just to the edge of the stream.

The twigs of his blind brushed against the thin legs of a flamingo that towered above him. The flamingo moved arrogantly downstream, shoving others that were drinking nearby. The *rogambi* came to view again. Moya watched while a great black foot placed itself squarely over the bell. Moya did not take his eyes from the flamingo's foot. He moved out into the water, first his face, then his body partly submerging in the stream. It was like entering a grove of pink trees. A rosy flamingo feather floated past his nose.

Replacing the contented rasping of the drinking flamingoes, a note of annoyance sounded as Moya crowded out first one, then another. The displaced flamingoes flapped their wings and crowded all the others back up the opposite shore.

Moya's hand shot out as the web foot upon which his eye was riveted moved along with the crowd. His hand slid swiftly over the *rogambi* as the foot moved off. Immediately, another web foot stomped down upon Moya's hand, which tried to grip the bell. The flamingo moved his foot, flapped his wings and squawked. Hopping and flapping restlessly, the flamingoes stirred about. Moya felt the air from their big wings as he slid his screen of branches back to the shore. The smell of dry soda clung to the flamingoes' feathers. Across the lake, a few flamingoes took off, rising against the sharp blue of the sky.

Moya relaxed with relief, and lay flat for a moment with the bell clutched in his hand.

"Nice going," Peter whispered.

Moya eased himself and his leafy screen to an upright position.

"We have to get to the cave," Moya told him softly. "The sun is getting hot. You must rest."

The boys crept away in their blinds. The flamingoes continued to drink, not noticing.

11: Blood Brothers

PETER HAD FORGOTTEN HIS WOUNDS IN HIS EXCITEMENT AT THE
search for the bell and the magnificence of the firebirds. As
they headed back to the cave, still covered by their leafy
screens, he whispered enthusiastically to Moya: "If my dad
could only get here with his movie camera, he could show
all this to his students."

Moya felt pride and happiness. His birds, the totem of his
clan, were a thing of wonder and beauty and excitement to
those from a far-off land. How far, he could not imagine. It
must be past the opposite wall of the Rift Valley, and past
the Kingdom of the Buganda, and the huge Lake Victoria
of which he had heard.

"My dad took us to the islands off Florida, and we could
hardly find any flamingoes," Peter told Moya. "They had
been scared away by airplanes flying over to look at them.
He took us to some swamps in France, and the flamingoes
there were great, but they were nothing like *this*. My dad

62

will crack up when he sees this. He has showed me pictures of the flamingoes that live in the mountain lakes in South America, and some place in India, but these are the best in the world."

The soaring pride in Moya's heart sank to fear. How could Peter's dad see it, when it was the secret of their clan? Moya's many troubles crashed upon him again. He saw that Peter's eyes were unnaturally bright, that he was weak, and staggered under his load of branches.

The boys had reached the shrubbery slope leading to their cave. They shed their leaves, Moya walking beside Peter to give him support.

"You'll have to rest now," Moya told Peter, rearranging the bed of leaves. When Peter was settled upon it, he looked at him anxiously.

"You know that I am in trouble."

"Yes, about the bell. But now you've found it. Everything's okay."

"Not everything, for I have let you look upon the Lake of the Firebirds, which is a secret place of our clan. You may get worse because of it, or something bad might befall my village. It is an evil which must be made right. There's no time to spare. Someone is sick in my village maybe because of this. I must leave to return the *gethiito* and the *rogambi*. But first, you and I must be blood brothers. That's the only way I can make things right."

Peter thought.

"Would that make my dad a blood dad, too, so he could see the lake?"

Moya scratched his head.

"I guess he would be a clan member if you were. But anyway, you and I must be blood brothers right now if I'm to get myself out of trouble."

Moya found the coffee pods in a corner of the cave. He handed one to Peter. They broke them open, and then they took Moya's knife. Moya found a place on his arm where the skin was soft and he could draw some blood from it.

"When in Rome, do as the Romans do," Peter said, shrugging his shoulders and following Moya's example. The boys gulped the coffee beans that had their blood mingled on them.

"Now we have to put our weapons behind us," Moya ex-

plained. He brought Peter's bow and arrow, placing it behind Peter. He sat with his knife behind him.

"We will never use weapons against one another, for we
are brothers," Moya announced. "Now we feast to cele-
brate." He peeled the leaves from the hot yams, and brought
other leaves so they could hold them without burning their
hands.

Peter cracked open the skin of the yam, and a cloud of
sweet-smelling steam arose. The boys ate the smooth orange
pulp greedily.

"Now I'm going." Moya took the bell, the horn and the
mask.

"Aren't you scared? What will he do to you for taking
those?"

"It doesn't matter what he'll do. I have to return them
because he needs them. If they let me come back, I'll bring
you some fresh milk and more ointment for your legs."

"What happens if you don't come back? What do I do?"

"I'll send Kimani, my brother. He will care for you."

"Send for my dad," urged Peter.

12: Captured

MOYA TRUDGED UP THE CLIFFS TOWARD HIS VILLAGE. THE clapper of the *rogambi* struck hollowly against the sides as he held the bell cupped in his hands and tried to plan what he would say to the mondo-mogo.

Passing his bird-scaring platform, he noticed that no one was there, and birds were in the millet field. Moya decided that once his problems were solved, he would volunteer to stay on the platform every day until the millet was harvested, without straying off once. He wished he were there now, that he had stuck to bird-scaring, and had never had the ambition to be a doctor, but then he would never have met Peter.

Moya picked up a rock, tossing it into the field. The little yellow birds flew off.

Moya heard branches move in the trees beside the millet field. As the branches parted, he saw the excited face of Mobura peering through.

"Come on, gang! I've found him!" Mobura shouted.

He approached Moya, but Moya started running.

Mobura and his friends were much bigger than Moya. Their legs were so much longer than Moya's that they overtook him, surrounding him.

"We caught him with the goods on him," Mobura boasted, flicking his fingers against the magic powder horn. "We are going to march you straight to the mondo-mogo, who is busy trying to make some new magic powder to replace what you stole, so that he can cure the grandfather of Murumba."

It was useless for Moya to try to talk. Mobura's boastful words went on and on until Moya wanted to clap his hands over his ears.

"I am head of a search party to find you, and it seems that they made a good choice, since I am bringing back the thief and the goods he stole, and lucky for you that Murumba's grandfather has not died—or he had not when we last heard—the consequences will be bad enough."

The bigger boys were walking in a tight formation around Moya, who looked very small among them. But when the boys passed a group of children playing at spear the hoop, they plucked Moya out from their midst.

"See we have caught your companion, Moya, who stole the *rogambi* and the *gethiito* from the mondo-mogo."

One of Moya's friends, his hand poised with a sharpened stick which he was about to throw in a hoop, turned a glance of scorn toward Moya.

The others stopped their game. The hoop rolled over on

its side and lay flat, and no one tried to spear it. The players looked toward Moya, and then away.

Moya wished that he was one of the players imprisoned by the other team, instead of being a captive of Mobura and his cruel friends. Nothing was worse than to be shunned by your age grade. Tears burned at the back of Moya's eyes, but he would not let them come out. He held his head very straight, and tried to ignore Mobura's endless stream of chatter.

He turned his thoughts toward his patient, back in the cave. Suppose that the clan was displeased with Moya? What would happen to Peter? He would probably be left in the cave with no food or care, and he might die.

Maybe they would not believe that Peter was a blood brother of the clan, because Moya was too small to be taken seriously.

Mobura gabbed on: "Your father will probably be fined. Perhaps thirty sheep or goats and a fat ram for the judges. But who knows? No one has ever before done anything so bad as to steal the mondo-mogo's magic.

"And what will your brother say—the great Kimani, who thinks he is going to be *muthamaki?* He will be in disgrace, along with you." Mobura's tongue never stopped.

Moya suddenly broke from the bigger boys and scuttled away, dashing with all the speed he could muster toward the hut of the witch doctor. His angered captors rushed after him, but Moya remained ahead, tumbling through the hut door, sprawling before the mondo-mogo.

"I have brought back your mask and your *rogambi* and the

magic horn," he gasped. "I am sorry you needed them. I needed them, too."

Mobura blustered in on Moya's heels.

"Brought them back! What a lie! He would not have come here if I and my friends had not captured him with the stolen magic and forced him back. This thief should be punished!" demanded Mobura.

The mondo-mogo frowned. The angry words of Mobura were not fitting for a boy to use in the presence of such a wise man as the mondo-mogo. The witch doctor took the magic articles from Moya, and fixed Mobura with such a piercing stare that Mobura shrunk a few inches back out the door of the hut.

"It is only the Council of Elders which judges whether a person is a liar or a thief," he admonished Mobura.

"Then I will tell them how I found Moya with the stolen goods," Mobura insisted.

"After I have visited my patient," the mondo-mogo said, gathering his masks and equipment. "Meanwhile, I will turn Moya over to his father."

The mondo-mogo walked toward Moya's father's house, leaving Mobura angry and disappointed that he had not seen Moya punished on the spot.

13: The Trial

THE KIAMA, THE FAMILY COUNCIL, MET IN THE LATE AFTER-noon. They were the oldest and the wisest men of Moya's clan. They sat in a circle, where one of the oldest poured sugar-cane beer and asked the spirits of their ancestors to join them. Then they turned toward the mountain where Ngai, their god, lived, and asked him to bring harmony to their family, but bad luck to anyone who did not agree with the decision the council reached.

Kimani stood with Moya, who was accused of stealing the mondo-mogo's magic. When the elders were ready to hear Moya's story, Moya hesitated, gripping in his hand the twigs with which he was to plead his case. Kimani felt his hesitation, and pressed his arm warmly about him, pushing him forward.

"Remember. Just be honest. You have nothing to hide."

Moya stepped woodenly into the circle. His face was so serious and he was so small that some of the elders smiled.

The mondo-mogo stood near the sacred fig tree that marked the trial place. His face was like a mask, yet Moya felt there was no anger in him, for he had defended him against Mobura. Moya could see the scornful face of Mobura out beyond the circle of judges.

Moya had already talked to Kimani, and they had decided where he would start.

"I was walking near the Lake of the Firebirds," Moya began. "I saw a boy overcome by the sun lying on the white part of the shore. He was very sick."

Mobura's haughty look changed to one of surprise.

"Who was this boy?" a judge asked Moya. "Was he a stranger?"

"Not a stranger. I had seen him before. He bought my sister's basket from me on the road to Nakuru. He was from a far-off land."

A murmur of concern ran through the assemblage. A stranger at the Lake of the Firebirds! This must be the American about whom the park ranger from Nakuru had inquired yesterday!

Kimani gave Moya a reassuring glance.

"He helped me, and he needed help. So I rolled him from the sun into a shady cave. He was very sore. He needed to be doctored. I went to the mondo-mogo, who gave me some ointment, but he was in a hurry, so I could not ask him for anything else. I had to borrow the *rogambi* and the horn and a mask so that I could properly cure my friend."

Moya described the way he had performed the ceremonies

and treated the wounds. The medicine man's face remained mask-like, but surprise radiated from his eyes.

Moya uncertainly held out a twig. He knew that he was supposed to offer the council of elders one of his twigs each time he had made a point for himself.

"Why did you not tell your parents, or some of us?"

"I was afraid my friend, not being of our clan, might come to harm for looking on the Lake of the Firebirds."

Some of the elders looked troubled. "Then you knew that this was a forbidden thing?"

Moya held out another stick. "Yes, but I have made it right. He is not a stranger now, but one of our clan."

Displaying the scratch on his arm, Moya continued: "We

have become blood brothers. The firebirds are his totem as well as ours. He protects them as we do, and they protect him."

One of the elders took the twig from Moya. All of the elders looked puzzled, as if they had never heard such a case before.

Mobura, trembling with rage, for he had seen the brotherly glances that passed from his rival, Kimani, sending strength to Moya, lunged forward.

"I want to tell how I captured him. He would not have brought the *rogambi* back if I had not caught him and dragged him here."

The head elder, who held Moya's twigs, fixed Mobura with a stern stare. "What do you say to that?" he asked Moya.

"I was on my way here. I was almost to the mondo-mogo's hut to return his things when I met Mobura," Moya told him. He handed over a third.twig.

The head elder said that they had heard Moya's story and they must settle the case quickly, because officials were looking for the sick boy.

A few were chosen from the circle of elders to decide whether Moya must pay a fine for wrongdoing, and these men went away to a secret grove to discuss Moya's story.

Moya looked at his father as he waited beside Kimani. He did not want his father to give up any sheep or goats because of him. His thoughts turned to Peter. What would happen to Peter if these men decided Moya had not done a good thing? Peter had lain a long time in the cave. He needed food. He needed fresh ointment. He needed someone to keep him from being lonely.

Moya thought of the flamingoes, the great pink garden upon the nesting grounds, the hubbub of their voices as they fed, the sweep of their flight over the lake. He thought of Peter's eager eyes devouring every motion. No, he was not lonely. Then Moya began to worry that Peter would go back to the lake again, and would break open his wounds.

Soon the council came back. The presiding judge held up Moya's twigs, announcing, his gaze riveted upon Mobura, that a curse would fall upon the fields and homestead of anyone who disagreed with the decision of the elders.

"We have found that Moya has followed well the rules of his clan according to his age grade, and the ancestral spirits are pleased with his observations of the customs and traditions of our clan. No fine is imposed upon the father of Moya. Moya is directed to take the mondo-mogo to his patient, and Kimani, his brother, is asked to travel to Nakuru to find those who search for Moya's blood brother, the new member of our clan."

The spectators cheered, and prepared to have a celebration. Mobura managed a weak smile. He did not want bad luck to fall upon his household.

14: Peter Disappears

"HE NEEDS MORE OINTMENT OF THE KIND YOU GAVE ME BE-
fore," Moya told the mondo-mogo. They secured the ointment, and Moya filled his basket with paw-paws and other
food.

Moya led the way. Nightfall was near, and they had to
hurry through the ravines and over the rocks.

"So you are determined to be a mondo-mogo, Moya?" the
medicine man asked.

"Yes, that is what I have always wanted."

"You must go to school, Moya," the wise old man told the
boy. "I can teach you things I know. But the world is chang-
ing. Iron birds bring medicine men from far away."

"The boy I found came from far away."

"Yes. These doctors have new medicines and ways of
healing. A good mondo-mogo collects all the wisdom he can.
You must learn the new ways, as well as the old, so that our
clan will have the best of mondo-mogos."

Moya hoped that when the witch doctor saw his patient, he would be proud of the way he had treated him. He led the way eagerly to the cave, parting the leleshwa bushes to make a path for the mondo-mogo.

As they stepped through the shrubs that screened the cave, Moya called to Peter: "I'm back. Everything is all right."

No answer came. Moya stepped into the cave.

"He's not here!" Moya exclaimed.

The mondo-mogo looked curiously about the cave. He examined the bushes to see in what direction the branches had been broken.

"We've been crashing all around here," Moya said. "I don't think we could track him."

"Where would he go?" asked the medicine man. "Back to his father? To look for you?"

"No. He's too smart for that. He knows he's sick. Maybe he's gone to look for food. I was gone a long time, and he had nothing but a couple of paw-paws around the cave."

"There's no food around here," observed the mondo-mogo. "Unless he eats flamingo eggs, as some of the other tribes do."

"No. He has pledged not to harm the flamingo."

Moya remembered the excited light in Peter's eyes that morning when they had watched the flamingoes at close range. Searching about the cave, he found Peter's basket, partly empty. There were many papers in the basket. They were covered with drawings of flamingo feet, feathers, wing positions, and other details. Moya saw that the big binoculars and Peter's camera were gone, and also his bow and arrow.

Moya tried to guess the probable route Peter had taken. He started toward the nesting colony with the mondo-mogo at his heels. As they walked down the lake shore, they could see, where the water had receded, many circles of dried mud, the rings left by the flamingoes as they rotated their beaks on the lake bottom, searching for food.

As they neared the nesting promontory, Moya and the mondo-mogo lowered themselves to the ground, creeping silently toward the feathery mass of pink with the forest of stick-like legs and the undulating curves of beak and neck towering toward the sky. When they were at a point of the shore just opposite the nesting colony, they saw the birds mirrored in the water of the lake. Moya noticed how the birds on the nests had folded those long, brittle-looking legs tightly to the sides of the nest.

Moya's glances about the edges of the lake revealed an unnatural mound of dry vegetation. A grin appeared on Moya's face. He nudged the mondo-mogo silently and pointed.

As the mondo-mogo looked, the dry mound of branches stirred, and almost imperceptibly moved.

Moya had to use all his self-control to keep from laughing.

The mound of leaves slithered away from the nesting colony inch by inch. Moya and the medicine man crawled toward it until they converged with it on the route to the cave. When they were at a safe distance from the nesting colony, Peter shucked off his branches. He had his binoculars strapped around one shoulder, and his bow and a quiver of arrows around the other. He shook off the bow and held it in his hand.

"This is the real mondo-mogo," Moya grinned.

"Is everything okay? You're not in trouble?"

"No, everything is good. The sick man has been doctored. The clan accepts you as a member. Kimani, my brother, has gone to find your father."

"Hooray!" shouted Peter.

"Your patient doesn't look very sick," remarked the mondo-mogo. But he frowned when he saw Peter's wounds, which were sore again from crawling.

Peter's eyes danced.

"Wait till I tell Dad what's here! At the same time, you can see nests being built, chicks hatching, and chicks going off on their own.

"I think I got some good pictures. I got one of the chicks just pecking its way through the shell, with my telescopic lens. He was all wet, with big pink feet that stuck up in front of him. He looked like he was sitting on his elbows. I even saw this newborn flamingo getting some kind of a drink out of its mother's beak.

"I watched this chick while it dried and learned to stand on its feet and walk. And in about an hour, it walked off its nest and had a swim and got together with some other baby chicks. The chicks got all mixed up in a big crowd! I wonder if that mother flamingo could figure out which one was her own chick!"

Moya translated all this for the mondo-mogo, and as he finished there was a rustle in the shrubbery. The three turned quickly to see a wild pig scurry through the brush. Peter whipped an arrow from his quiver, set it in his bow and let it fly.

"Zap!" It hit its mark.

"It's that pig I was chasing, I'll bet," said Moya.

"That pig could have gone down to the nesting colony for flamingo eggs," Peter said. They ran to examine the pig.

"The pig is just right for a feast," said the mondo-mogo.

"Let's build our fire up well and have a roast," Moya suggested, making for the cave, and picking up bits of branches as he ran.

"That's not the first arrow I've used today," said Peter. "I caught a fish eagle dive-bombing some flamingo chicks. I had to let him have it, but it was pretty hard to aim without moving my blind too much."

Again Moya translated for the mondo-mogo. The mondo-mogo said that Peter was a good protector of the clan totem.

When the boys and the witch doctor were in the cave, Moya built up the fire, and the doctor examined Peter's wounds.

"Is he going to do some more ceremonies?" Peter asked Moya.

"No, you only do those once. He's just going to put some more ointment on your wounds, and he says for you to lie still for a while and be quiet."

Peter made a face. "It's too exciting around these flamingoes. I can't stand to miss anything. I hope your brother finds my dad. My dad will bring his microscope, and we can study the lake water and see what they eat. Dad says they must eat algae because of that blue color of the lakes."

"I thought they ate nothing," said Moya. "We have never seen any life in the lakes: no fish, no snails, and no plants."

"There are lots of plants in the water," Peter answered. "Only they're so small you don't see them. Diatoms, algae, all kinds of microscopic things. When Dad comes and we get up a lab, you'll see them on the slides."

Moya was puzzled by this, but it sounded interesting. He had been preparing the pig, and now he set up a spit of two forked sticks over the fire, impaling the pig on a third one. Soon the pig was sizzling. Drops of fat hissed into the fire and sent out a tantalizing aroma.

"Golly, I haven't had anything since breakfast," said Peter.

15: Reunion

THERE WAS A NOISE OF FOOTSTEPS. MOYA LOOKED OUT AND SAW Kimani through the screen of shrubs.

"Moya?" Kimani asked, guardedly.

"Yes, Kimani. We're here. Come in."

Kimani pushed aside the branches. Moya saw that he had three men with him.

The first one's eyes searched the flickers of firelight in the cave, and when they lit upon Peter, he darted forward, going down on his knees and embracing the boy with emotion.

"Dad! At last! Wait till you see what I've seen." Peter was breathless. His father laughed and hugged him again.

"I've brought a doctor from Nakuru, and this is Njiri, the ranger who's been helping me to search for nests. Only it looks like Peter led us to the end of the trail, eh, Njiri?"

The ranger smiled and nodded.

Moya felt warm inside. A big smile floated up from the warmth as he watched the happiness of father and son.

"This is our doctor," Kimani said, indicating the mondo-mogo.

The doctor from Nakuru began to examine Peter's wounds.

"It looks as if they were healing and you broke them open again," the doctor commented.

Moya giggled. Peter made a face.

"How can a person stay in a cave with flamingoes making fireworks all over the lake?" he asked.

"You must stay quiet," the doctor admonished.

"Well, now that Dad is here, I guess I can. I was afraid Dad would never get here, and I would have to see everything to report to him. See, Dad, I have made drawings of parts of the flamingoes that I have seen up close. Their beaks are different from some flamingoes that we have seen."

"Yes, these are the Lesser flamingoes," his father said. "They have shallower beaks than other varieties."

"What is the ointment you have been using?" the doctor asked the mondo-mogo. Moya translated as the mondo-mogo described it.

"The boy is in good shape. You've done a nice job," the doctor complimented the medicine man.

The mondo-mogo, though he could not speak the doctor's language, indicated by gestures that it was not he, but Moya who had done the healing.

"Yes, Dad, would you believe that this little kid found me konked out down by the lake in the sun and he dragged me up here and took care of me?"

The boys told the story of the past two days, and of how Peter had become a blood brother of the clan.

"We wonder if my dad is now in the clan, too?" Peter asked.

The witch doctor smiled, and said that it must be that a blood brother's father also belonged to the clan.

"I cured him with magic," Moya explained to Peter's father. "The magic bell and the magic horn."

The doctor from Nakuru looked thoughtful. "It's a good magic, the ringing of the *rogambi* and the ceremony of the horn and masks. For believing in their magic brings peace of mind to the person being healed, and this helps him to get well."

The aroma of the pig filled the cave.

Squawks, honks and cooing of the flamingoes floated up from the lake, and now and then the music of a flock moving from one feeding place to another sounded through the night.

Peter's father could not resist leaving the cave for a look at the lake, and even in the twilight, he was awed by the thousands of birds that milled, floated and stalked about the lake, or sat on the nesting promontory.

"You see, Dad, this lake is a secret, and the flamingoes are the totem of our clan," Peter explained. "Not many people know about it."

"With this great nesting colony that you describe," Njiri said, "we should take steps to make this a sanctuary, with some of your clan as rangers for it."

"Kimani!" Moya eagerly suggested. "He has always wanted to be a ranger."

"It's true. That's my ambition," Kimani confessed.

"Stay and help us now," Peter's father said. "We will get our gear set up here and pitch a camp. We've got lots of research to do, and you can help us make observations."

Moya watched the joy on his older brother's face.

"You stay, too, Moya, and take care of the patient," Peter's father added.

"I'm not going to be a patient much longer," Peter said. "I'm going to be down there making observations with the rest of you."

Suddenly Moya looked troubled.

"What about this doctor and ranger?" he asked. "Shall we make them blood brothers of the clan?"

Everybody laughed. "Moya has learned well his lessons about the rules and tradition of his clan," the mondo-mogo said. "There are many of our young people who do not bother to learn them nowadays."

When the pig was done, the doctors, the boys, and the scientists sat about the fire devouring the steaming pork and scooping out the soft pulp of paw-paws. They talked as they feasted, the ranger planning how they would make the Lake of the Firebirds a sanctuary to which passes would be limited to scientists during nesting time and over which airplanes would be forbidden to fly at that time.

Peter's father spoke of plans to keep the lake from drying up, for its level had dropped many feet over the centuries.

Moya, listening, crept into a shadowy corner away from the firelight, and filled with happiness that the blue lake of his clan would always glow with the radiance of the flamingoes, he fell asleep.